This book is a work of fiction. Any references to historical events, real people, or real places are used fictitiously. Other names, characters, places, and events are products of the author's imagination, and any resemblance to actual events or places or persons, living or dead, is entirely coincidental.

LITTLE SIMON
An imprint of Simon & Schuster Children's Publishing Division
1230 Avenue of the Americas, New York, New York 10020
Copyright © 2014 by Simon & Schuster, Inc.
All rights reserved, including the right of reproduction in whole or in part in any form.
LITTLE SIMON is a registered trademark of Simon & Schuster, Inc., and associated colophon is a trademark of Simon & Schuster, Inc.
For information about special discounts for bulk purchases, please contact
Simon & Schuster Special Sales at 1-866-506-1949
or business@simonandschuster.com.
The Simon & Schuster Speakers Bureau can bring authors to your live event.
For more information or to book an event contact the Simon & Schuster
Designed by Nicholas Sciacca and Emmy Reis
Speakers Bureau at 1-866-248-3049 or visit our website at www.simonspeakers.com.
Manufactured in the United States of America 0117 MTN
4 5 6 7 8 9 10
Library of Congress Cataloging-in-Publication Data
O'Ryan, Ray.
Drake makes a splash! / by Ray O'Ryan ; illustrated by Colin Jack.
pages cm. — (Galaxy Zack ; 8)
Summary: When summer arrives on Nebulon, Zack discovers that his best friend
Drake is afraid to learn to swim and decides to teach him
before they go on a trip to water-covered planet Araxie.
ISBN 978-1-4424-9360-5 (pbk : alk. paper) — ISBN 978-1-4424-9361-2 (hc : alk. paper) —
ISBN 978-1-4424-9362-9 (ebook) [1. Science fiction. 2. Swimming—Fiction. 3. Fear—Fiction.
4. Outer space—Fiction.] I. Jack, Colin, illustrator. II. Title.
PZ7.O7843Dr 2014
[Fic]—dc23
2013020710

CONTENTS

Chapter 1
Heat Wave

Nebulon's two suns shone down brightly. Summer had come to the planet, and the temperature was close to 110 degrees.

And today was the coolest day in more than a week.

Zack Nelson walked down the main

street of Creston City with his friend Drake Taylor. Figuring out how to stay cool was getting harder and harder.

"We could go back to the indoor snow-slide and ride the slippo-discs down the mondo-hill again," Drake suggested.

"Nah, we did that yesterday," Zack

pointed out. "What about going swimming in the Nebu-Dome?"

The Nebu-Dome was a recreation
center. It had a running track, ball
courts, and a big pool.

"I do not think so," replied Drake.

"Well, we have to do *something*,"

said Zack. "I can't take much more of this heat. Even the stripe-o-dils are wilting!"

Zack pointed to a patch of flowers. Each flower was shaped like a rose, but was covered in black and white stripes like a zebra. The stripe-o-dils

usually loved the heat, but now they were bent over, leaning toward the ground. They looked as if they were searching for a cool drink of water.

Then Zack spied something up ahead that made his eyes open wide.

"Look!" he said, pointing to a sign in front of the Creston Vivi-Theater. "There's a new vivi-vid playing. We're saved!"

5

Vivi-vids were special movies made on Nebulon. Zack had seen 3-D movies back on Earth, but vivi-vids took the 3-D experience to a whole new level. They made those watching them feel like they were part of the movie.

"White-Water Wonders!" said Zack, reading the sign. The image showed two Nebulites in a thin metal raft zooming through a raging river.

"Perfect!" cried Zack. "Putting ourselves into a white-water adventure on a river should cool us right off!"

Zack hurried toward the theater entrance. A few seconds later he realized that Drake was trailing behind him. Zack waited for Drake to catch up.

"What's wrong, Drake?" he asked. "Don't you think this is a good idea?"

"Well . . ." Drake paused. "Maybe."

"Of course it is!" said Zack. "Come on!"

"Okay, I guess," said Drake.

I wonder what's up with Drake, Zack thought. Then the two friends walked into the vivi-theater.

Chapter 2

WHITE-WATER WONDERS!

Zack and Drake stopped at the snack stand. They each bought a bag of roasted nebu-nuts, their favorite snack. Then Zack led them to two seats near the front of the theater.

"Do we have to sit so close to the screen?" asked Drake.

"The closer we sit, the more it'll feel like we're actually in the raft going down the river," Zack explained.

"Uh . . . going down the river?" Drake asked nervously.

"Sure, isn't that the whole point?"

asked Zack. "This should really cool us off!"

The vivi-theater went dark. Suddenly a rush of water seemed to pour from the screen. Within seconds Zack and Drake were swept up in the vivi-vid.

They felt as if they
were racing down
white-water rapids.
"Weeeee-iiiii!"
screamed Zack.

Drake slouched
down in his seat and
held his head with his
hands. Each time the raft
bounced over a wave, he
let out a frightened cry.

In between laugh-
ing and screaming,
Zack turned to Drake.

"Isn't this great?"

cried Zack. "I'm cooler already."

That's when Zack noticed the look of fear on Drake's face.

"Are you okay, buddy?" asked Zack.

"Yeah," Drake replied, forcing a smile. "I am just not used to this."

The raft flew into the air. For a few
seconds, Zack felt weightless. Then he
splashed back down into the river.

"Yah-ha!" shouted Zack.

Drake turned away from the screen.

When the vivi-vid ended, the boys stepped back outside into the scorching heat.

"That was grape!" said Zack.

Drake walked along quietly.

"What's wrong?" Zack asked.

"Nebulites do not really like water," Drake explained. "We do not like to swim. And we would never go on a raft down a river. Even when it is really hot."

Zack felt the heat of the Nebulon suns beating down on top of his head.

"But there were lots of Nebulites

in the vivi-theater, Drake," Zack said.
"They all seemed to be having a great
time."

Drake just looked away and
shrugged.

Something's up with Drake, Zack
thought. *There's something he's not
telling me!*

Chapter 3
A Chance for Relief

When Zack arrived home, he fell into a soft chair in the living room. He was covered in sweat and his face was red.

Otto Nelson looked at his son. "Did you just run around Creston City?" asked Zack's dad.

"All I did was walk home from the

vivi-theater," Zack explained. "It's so hot that by my third step I was already wiped out."

"Did you see a good vivi-vid?"

"Yeah!" exclaimed Zack. "It was grape. All about riding a raft down a river. I felt cool for a little while. Then I stepped outside and got hot all over again."

"Hey, I've got an idea," said Dad. "Why don't we plan a family trip to Araxie? Almost the entire planet is covered with water. There are plenty of great places to swim, and the temperature on Araxie is always cooler than on Nebulon. You can ask Drake to join us too."

Zack jumped up from the chair.

"That's a great idea!"

"I'll speak with Mom, and we'll figure out when to go."

"Thanks, Dad!" Zack dashed to his bedroom.

"Vid-chat with Drake, please, Ira," he said.

"Certainly, Master Just Zack."

24

A few seconds later Drake's face appeared on a giant screen. The screen took up most of a wall of Zack's bedroom.

"Master Drake for you," announced Ira.

"Thanks, Ira," said Zack.

"Hi, Zack," said Drake.

"How would you like to go on a trip with my family to Araxie?" asked Zack. "The whole planet is covered in water. We could swim all day and cool right off!"

"Uh . . . I do not know," Drake said.

Zack stared at his friend's face on the big screen. He thought that Drake looked a little bit scared.

"Are you okay, Drake?" Zack finally asked. "You're acting a little weird today."

"You promise that you will not make fun of me?" asked Drake.

"I promise," replied Zack.

"The truth is," Drake began slowly, "I lied when I said that all Nebulites do not like water and swimming. It is just me. I am too afraid to learn how to swim!"

Chapter 4
Swimming Lessons

"Wow!" exclaimed Zack. "No wonder you didn't like that vivi-vid. All my
friends back on Earth loved to swim. I
never thought that you may not like it."

Drake looked very disappointed. "I
am sorry, Zack," said Drake. "Maybe
you should go to Araxie without me."

"Wait a minute," said Zack. "I have an idea! *I* can teach you how to swim. Then you won't be afraid, and you can come with us!"

Drake looked scared. "I do not know," he said.

"Just try it," suggested Zack. "If you don't like it, we'll stop."

"Well . . ."

"Just one time," said Zack. "How about that?"

"Oh, okay," Drake said. "One time."

"Grape! You can come over tomorrow and we can start."

Zack bounded into and then out of the elevator and ran to find his dad.

Otto was at his desk, scanning through the giant 3-D web-screen on the wall. He was researching family vacations on Araxie.

"Hey, Dad. Do we still have that kiddie pool I used when I learned how to swim?" he asked.

"Yup. Why?"

"Drake told me that he doesn't

know how to swim!" Zack explained. "I thought I would teach him. We could start in that pool."

"Great idea!" said Dad. "Come on, I'll help you set it up."

Chapter 5
SPLASH!

The next morning, Drake arrived at the Nelsons' house.

"Good morning, Master Drake," said Ira as the front door swung open. "Master Just Zack is in the backyard."

"Thanks, Ira," said Drake.

Drake walked through the house

and out the back door. As he stepped into the backyard, Drake saw a yellow kiddie pool.

"Water please, Ira," said Zack. A small panel in the side of the house slid open. Out popped a hose. It quickly filled up the pool.

From out of nowhere, Luna, the Nelsons' dog, bounded into the backyard. She jumped right into the middle of the pool!

KER-SPLASH!

Water spurted up over the sides!

"Luna, . . ."

". . . the pool . . ."

". . . is not ready yet!" said Charlotte
and Cathy, Zack's twin sisters.

Luna sloshed around the pool. Then she jumped out and shook her fur. Water sprayed everywhere. Zack, Drake, and the girls got soaked.

"My clothes are all wet," said Drake, wiping his hands on his wet shirt. "Maybe I should go home. I can learn to swim another time. Besides, I do not have a bathing suit."

Just then Zack's mom stepped out
of the house. She was holding one of
Zack's bathing suits. "Problem solved,"
she said.

"Uh, thanks, Mrs. Nelson," Drake said. But Drake did not sound happy about getting the bathing suit. He headed inside to change.

Drake came out a few minutes later.

He walked slowly to the edge of the pool. When he peered into the water, a look of terror spread across his face.

"There's nothing to be scared of, Drake," said Zack. "The water is not that deep. Come on, don't be such an Umba bird!"

Umba birds were common on Nebulon. They were known for being easily frightened.

Drake stepped away from the pool and shook his head.

"I do not think I can do this," he said sadly.

Chapter 6
Helping Hands

"Zack, can I talk to you for a moment please?" Mom called from the house.

Zack hurried inside.

"It's not nice to call Drake names," Mom said firmly.

"But the water isn't even deep!" whined Zack.

x

45

"You need to have patience with your friend. Do you remember the first time Dad and I tried to teach *you* to swim?"

Zack nodded. "I remember. I cried *forever.*"

"That's right," said Mom. "But because your dad and I showed you patience, you found the courage to try again. And now . . ."

"I love swimming," Zack said, finishing Mom's thought.

"Drake will never find the confidence to enjoy swimming if you make fun of him." Mom pointed out at the pool. "Look at that," she said.

Zack looked back at the pool. He saw that Charlotte and Cathy had brought a pair of old floaties out of

the garage. They had put a floatie on
each of Drake's arms.

"Now step into the pool . . . ,"
Charlotte said to Drake.

". . . slowly," added Cathy.

The girls each stood on either side
of Drake for support.

Drake slowly lifted his left foot and
stepped into the pool.

"Now the other one," said Charlotte.

A look of fear spread across
Drake's face.

"It's okay," Cathy said softly. "You can do it."

Drake put his other foot into the pool.

"Great!" said Charlotte. The two girls stepped into the pool beside Drake.

"Now lower yourself down into the water," said Cathy.

Drake hesitated. Then he sat down in the pool. His frightened look soon changed into a smile. He started splashing water over himself and at the girls. Everyone laughed.

Zack turned to his mom. "You're right. I should help Drake, not call him names."

Zack ran back outside. "Drake!" he called out. "I'm sorry I called you an Umba bird. That wasn't nice."

"Thanks, Zack," said Drake. "I feel better now that Charlotte and Cathy have helped me."

"Would you mind some company in the pool?" asked Zack.

"The more the merrier!" said Drake.
Zack jumped into pool, creating a
big splash.

Then Luna raced across the yard.
She leaped into the pool, sending
water flying everywhere.

Chapter 7
The Deep End

Drake went over to Zack's house every day for the next few days. Each day, he played in the kiddie pool. And each time, he felt a little more comfortable being in the water.

"So how's Drake doing with his swimming?" Dad asked one day at dinner.

"He likes . . ."

". . . being in . . ."

". . . the pool," said the twins.

"But it's not exactly swimming," added Zack. "I really want to help him learn to swim in deeper water so he can come with us to Araxie."

"Hmmm . . . ," said Dad, scratching his head. "Maybe we can take him to the Nebu-Dome's big pool."

"Grape!" shouted Zack. "I'll let him know."

The next day, Dad, Zack, and Drake climbed into Dad's flying car. They sped off to the Nebu-Dome. Drake's floaties and a large inner tube were stuffed into the backseat beside the boys.

"I am a little nervous about swimming in a big pool," Drake admitted.

"There's nothing to worry about," said Zack. "I'll be there to help you."

Drake nodded and stared out the window. He remained quiet for the rest of the trip.

A few minutes later, they were at the Nebu-Dome. From the outside, it looked like a giant flying saucer.

Dad eased the front of his flying

car into a garage inside the Nebu-
Dome. A green flashing light on the
dashboard told him that the car was
locked in place.

Zack, Dad, and Drake climbed out
of the car. Drake reached back into
the car and grabbed the floaties and
the inner tube.

A platform carried the group into

the Nebu-Dome's main building. Once inside, the platform became a moving sidewalk. It took them past many Nebulites exercising and playing.

They passed a track where the runners ran a few feet above the ground, on a cushion of air. They glided by a large room filled with pulse-ball courts.

Players battled to control a glowing metal ball. They then tossed the ball through a moving, flashing hoop.

The group finally came to the pool. They stepped off the moving sidewalk and saw many Nebulites splashing, swimming, and having a great time.

"Come on," said Zack. "Let's join

them!" Zack peeled off his shirt and shoes. He raced to the pool and jumped right in.

Drake walked slowly to the edge of the pool. He slipped one floatie onto each arm. Then he placed the inner tube into the water.

"Come on in, Drake," Zack called

out. He treaded water a few feet from the edge.

Drake sat on the edge, and then he dropped into the shallow water.

"Use the inner tube to hold you up," suggested Dad.

Drake clung to the edge of the pool.

"It's okay," said Zack, trying to

encourage his friend. "Just swim toward me."

"What is wrong, Drake? Afraid of a little water?" said someone from behind Zack.

"Seth!" cried Zack.

Seth Stevens, the bully from school, was swimming toward Drake.

Chapter 8
Drake, the Swimmer

Zack swam quickly, putting himself between Seth and Drake.

"Drake is learning how to swim, Seth," said Zack. "You making fun of him is not going to help!"

"What is so hard about swimming?" Seth shouted at Drake.

Seth had gotten nicer toward Zack since the first time they met. But sometimes he still acted like a bully.

"What's so scary about dogs, Seth?" Zack asked. "Remember the first time you met Luna? You were so scared of her. I had to show you that there was nothing to be afraid of."

"Uh, yeah, I remember," Seth said.

"Well, I'm doing the same for Drake with swimming," Zack explained.

"I guess so," Seth said, shrugging. Then he turned and swam away.

"Thanks, Zack," said Drake.

"No problem," said Zack. "Now, grab the inner tube. Come on—you can do it!"

Drake moved one hand from the side of the pool and put it on the inner tube. Then he took a deep breath and moved his other hand. He floated away from the edge.

"Great! Now kick your feet!" said Zack.

Drake stretched out and started kicking his feet. He sliced through the water, moving across the pool. Zack swam beside him.

Drake reached the other side of the pool. He let go of the tube and grabbed the edge.

"Great job, Drake!" said Zack.

Drake practiced swimming with the tube for the rest of the afternoon.

"Good start, buddy," said Zack. "Let's come back tomorrow."

After a couple of days, Mr. Nelson wanted Drake to move on to the next level as a swimmer.

"Ready to put that inner tube aside?" he asked.

"Well, I am not sure, Mr. Nelson," said Drake, looking worried.

"You've still got the floaties on your arms," Zack reminded his friend, "and I'll be swimming right beside you."

"Okay," Drake finally said. "I will try."

Dad reached down and pulled the inner tube out of the water. Drake took a deep breath, then pushed off.

"Big strokes!" Zack called out as he swam beside him.

Drake reached out with each arm and pulled back through the water. He kicked his feet as he went.

"I did it!" he shouted when he reached the other side. A big smile spread across his face.

Mr. Nelson took Zack and Drake back to the Nebu-Dome every day. By the middle of the second week, Zack thought it was time for Drake to take off the floaties.

Chapter 9
Ready for Araxie!

Drake looked nervous. He slowly took the floaties off his arms. Then he swam back across the pool.

There was no doubt about it. Drake was now a swimmer!

"You're swimming like a champ, Drake," said Dad.

"Thanks, Mr. Nelson. You and Zack are a big help."

At the end of the second week, Zack could see that Drake was swimming with much more confidence.

"Hey, let's play ring dive!" Zack suggested. "I think Drake is ready for that."

"What is ring dive?" asked Drake.

"Watch!" said Dad.

Dad walked over to a control panel near the edge of the pool. He punched in a code. Suddenly, a large robotic arm dropped from the ceiling. A ring of flashing colors appeared at the end of the arm.

"The robot arm will toss the rings to different spots in the pool," Zack explained. "We each dive after the rings and try to catch them before they reach the bottom."

"Okay," said Drake.

"Ring dive . . . go!" shouted Zack.

The robotic arm tossed two colorful rings to opposite sides of the pool. Zack took off after the far ring. He dove beneath the pool's surface. He spotted

the flashing ring through the shimmering water. Zack swam hard and reached the ring. Then he grabbed it and returned to the surface.

Meanwhile, Drake went after the closer ring. He kicked his feet and moved his arms, but he couldn't catch up to the ring. It ended up on the bottom of the pool.

Drake pushed himself back up to the surface and swam to the edge.

"I could not get it," he said, catching his breath.

"Try again," said Zack. "Ring dive . . . go!"

Two more flashing rings flew from the end of the robotic arm. This time Drake swam out as soon as he saw the ring move. He was able to reach it in a couple of strokes. He grabbed the colorful hoop.

"I got it!" Drake shouted as he splashed back up to the surface.

"Good job!" said Zack.

"I think you're ready to come with us to Araxie," said Mr. Nelson.

"Sounds like fun," Drake said, smiling. "When do we leave?"

Chapter 10
Beat the Heat

A few days later, Zack, Drake, Charlotte, Cathy, and Mr. and Mrs. Nelson piled into the family car. They headed to the Creston City Spaceport. Luna went along too.

"I can't wait to get away from all this heat!" said Zack.

"And we can't wait . . ."

". . . to see Drake swim!" said Cathy and Charlotte.

"I'm proud of you, Drake," said Mrs. Nelson. "You worked hard, you fought your fears, and now you can enjoy swimming."

Drake smiled. "I could not have done it without Zack," he said.

Zack watched as the car flew down toward the parking area of the space-port. Out in the big launching area, he saw a line of people waiting to board the shuttle to Araxie. Most of them wore bathing suits and carried masks and snorkels.

"Come on!" cried Zack. "We don't want to miss the shuttle!"

Dad eased the car into a parking dock. Everyone scrambled out and grabbed their things. Then they hurried aboard the shuttle.

Soon the
shuttle blasted
off. Zack settled
back in his seat. He looked out the
window at the stars whizzing by. Zack
felt happy. He always did when he
traveled in space.

"Are we . . ."

". . . almost there?" asked the twins.

"We just took off," Mom pointed out. "But we'll be there before you know it."

After breakfast, a bright ball appeared in the distance.

"It's so blue!" cried Zack.

"That's because Araxie is almost completely covered in water," Dad explained. "There are thousands of tiny islands scattered across the huge ocean."

"And we're going to be on one of them soon!" said Zack.

What looked like a tiny speck grew larger and larger. Then a small island came into view.

"That's where we're going to spend the next few days!" Dad announced.

"Time to beat the heat!"

After the shuttle landed, everyone hopped onto a space bus. It sped above the surface and brought them from the spaceport to the beach.

Floating above the sand was a series of small cabins.

Dad checked his hyperphone. "Cabin 12," he said. "That's us. That'll be our home for the next few days."

"The cabin floats in the air?" Zack asked.

"Yup," said Dad. "Not only that. It also travels from beach to beach all around Araxie. Each day we can visit a different beach. And when we're ready to eat or to sleep, our cabin will be right there!"

"Grape!" Zack and Drake said together.

Dad entered a code into his hyper-phone. Floating cabin number 12 drifted down and landed gently on the sand.

"Let's bring our luggage inside," said Mom. "Then we can hit the beach!"

After settling into their cabin, everyone stepped out onto the beach. The cabin rose back into the air.

All along the beach Araxites stretched out on blankets or played in the water. They were green-skinned and had webbing between their fingers. Their feet were flipper-like, perfect for living on a planet that was mostly water.

Mom spread out a heat-resistant blanket on the sand. Dad opened up a hover-brella, an umbrella that floated above the blanket. As the sun changed position, the hover-brella shifted to keep the blanket nice and shady.

Luna raced along the beach and dove into the ocean.

"Who wants a snack?" asked Mom.
She pressed a button on the ultra-
freeze cooler. The top slid open to
reveal cool drinks and snacks.

"Maybe later, Mom. We . . ."

". . . want to try out . . ."

". . . our new surf suits!" said the
twins.

Charlotte and Cathy each wore a
special suit that helped them ride on
waves. They charged into the ocean.
When a wave came along, they floated
on top of it, all the way to shore.

"Drake and I want to check out all
the cool Araxie fish," said Zack. He
and Drake grabbed their snorkeling

gear. Zack pointed to a cove just up the beach.

"I read on the ultra-web about that cove," Zack said. "It's known for having colorful fish."

"Okay," said Mom. "Have fun and be careful. And stay where I can see you."

The two boys walked to the cove.

Zack slipped on his snorkel gear
and plunged into the water.

"Ready to see some cool fish?" he
called back to Drake.

Drake put on his mask, snorkel, and flippers. He held his floaties and looked at the ocean stretching out before him.

"Zack, I am scared!" he said. "I . . . I cannot do this!"

Chapter 11
Araxie Vacation

"What do you mean, Drake?" Zack asked. "You've become an awesome swimmer."

"But the pool was different," Drake replied. He backed away from the water's edge. "The ocean is so big. And it goes on forever. And there are

no sides to hold on to."

Zack stepped out of the water and walked over to his friend.

"Remember how scared you were of our little kiddie pool?" he asked.

Drake nodded.

"But you got in and did really well, right?" Zack pointed out.

Again, Drake nodded.

"And then when we got to the big pool at the Nebu-Dome, you were scared all over again," Zack continued. "But you got into that pool and soon you were swimming without any tube or floaties."

"I know, Zack. But this is different."

"It's just bigger, that's all. And the water is really calm. Why don't you put your floaties on? That will help you relax."

"Okay," Drake said nervously. He slipped the floaties onto his arms.

Drake walked slowly toward the water's edge. Pausing for a moment, he stepped into the ocean.

When he had gotten
in up to his knees, he stopped again.

"Okay. You're doing great. Now
stretch out in the water," said Zack.

Drake took a deep breath. Then
slowly he lifted his legs. He floated
easily on the ocean's surface.

Zack was proud of his friend. "Good
job!" he said.

Peering through their masks into the clear water, the boys saw an amazing variety of fish. Some were huge and moved through the ocean like orange and blue submarines. Others were tiny and traveled in groups of hundreds, forming silver and gold waves under the surface.

A skinny purple fish with three heads paused beneath the boys. One head looked up at Zack. Another head looked right at Drake. The third head gobbled down a passing green-and-yellow fish.

After snorkeling for a while, the boys splashed their way out of the ocean.

"That was amazing, Zack!" said Drake. "Thanks for helping me learn to swim."

"Hey," said Zack. "What are friends for?"

Drake climbed onto a rock.

"Watch this!" he said.

Zack could tell that his friend was no longer afraid of the water.

Drake jumped off the rock. He landed in the ocean with a big splash. Out of nowhere, Luna appeared and jumped in after him.

Zack laughed and clapped his hands. "That was great!"

"Time for lunch, boys," called Mom. Everyone gathered on the beach. Dad entered the code into his hyperphone, and the cabin floated down to the sand.

"I just checked the weather report

for Nebulon," announced Mr. Nelson. "The Nebulon Weather Authority predicts that the heat wave will break by the time we get home."

"Yippee wah-wah!" said Zack.

"But whenever it gets hot again," said Drake, "I can just jump into the closest pool!"

GALAXY ZACK

ADVENTURE!

HERE'S A SNEAK PEEK!

"Dad's home!" Zack shouted, racing to the door. Shelly and the twins followed.

Next to Dad stood a four-foot-tall robot. It had a narrow body that looked like the shape of a dress, short legs, and long mechanical arms. A marble-shaped head sat above its body.

An excerpt from *The Annoying Crush*